D0193148

For Jonathan

Here are lots of simple rhymes,
and flaps for little fingers to lift.
It's a book for dipping into and
passing shared moments of
anticipation and delight
with your child.

Rod Campbell

Rod Campbell's

# Animal Book

MACMILLAN CHILDREN'S BOOKS

# Little Miss Muffet

Little Miss Muffet
Sat on a tuffet
Eating her curds and whey.
Down came a . . .

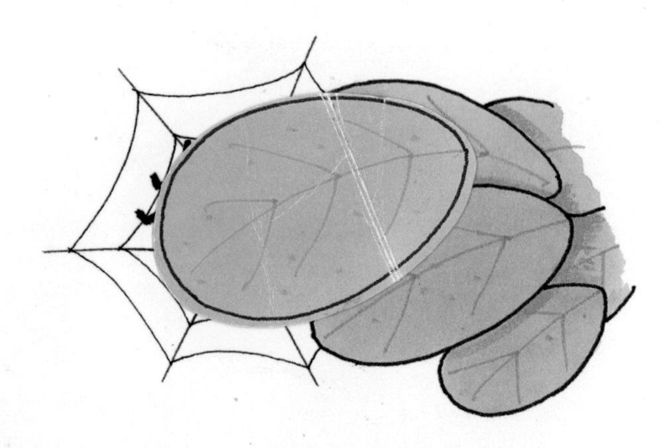

And sat down beside her
And frightened Miss Muffet away!

# The Bear Family

How many bears can you see?
Mummy, daddy, baby – three!

# Pet Shop Puppies

Four little puppies,
Want to come with me.
I took the white one home,
Then there were three.

Three little puppies,
What could I do?
I took the black one home,
Then there were two.

Two little puppies,
Playing in the sun.
I took the grey one home,
Then there was one.

One little puppy,
Looking very glum.
I took it home as well,
Then there were none!

Because, you see, they're all at home with me!

# The Rabbit

Tommy has a rabbit,
Its fur is soft and white.

It hops about all day,

And goes to sleep at night.

# Dicky Birds

Two little dicky birds,
Sitting on a wall,
One named Peter,
One named Paul.

Fly away, Peter,
Fly away, Paul,
Come back, Peter!
Come back, Paul!

# At the Zoo

At the zoo we saw someone very big,

and very small,

and very long,

and very tall!

There were three pretty parrots in a tree,

and a funny chimpanzee!

a lion, a tiger, a camel, too

(I ran past the lion – well, wouldn't you?)

There were lots of penguins, smartly dressed,

but I liked the . . .

. . . best!

# Our Pets

Sally has a tortoise,

Billy has a dog,

Katy has a rabbit,

And Freddy has a . . .

# Henry

Henry likes to play –
He can run around all day.

When it's time to have a rest,
Henry likes his basket best!

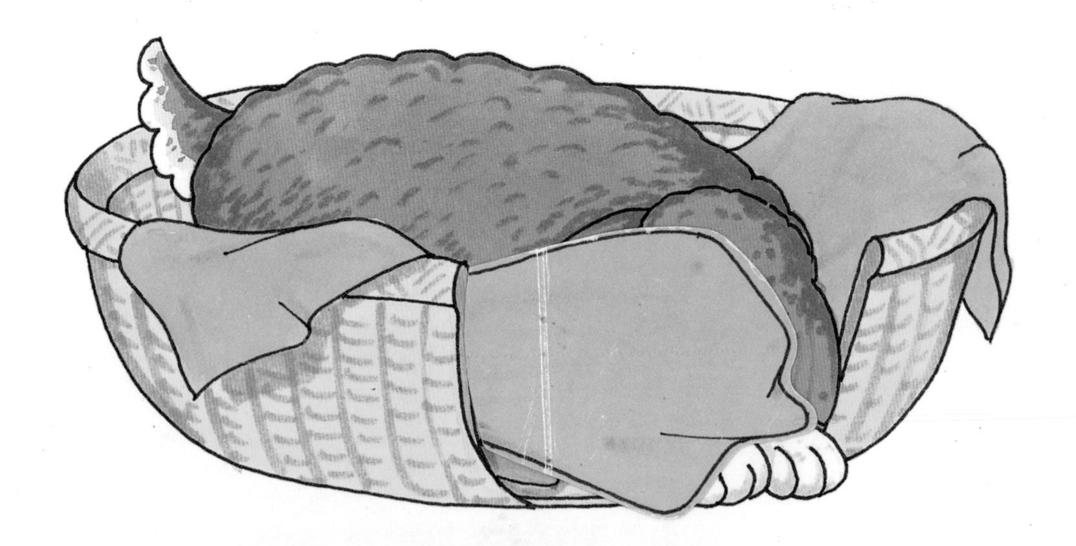

Is Henry asleep?
Go on, have a peep!

# Cat and Mouse

Kitty's running round the house,
She thinks she saw a little mouse.
There is a little mouse somewhere –
Perhaps he's underneath the chair?

Kitty stops and turns around,
Then creeps along without a sound.

But little mouse has run away,
So Kitty won't catch him today!

# The Pond

See the frogs,
Sitting, jumping,
Hippity, hoppity, hop!
They sit quite still,
Croaking, croaking,
Then, into the water,

# The Farm

Here's the farm.

In the barn there's a . . .

In the sty there's a . . .

In the stable there's a . . .

In the henhouse there's a . . .

But where's Sam, the farm dog?

Shh! He's asleep!

# Nesting Box

Little bird cannot speak,
She's got a worm in her beak.
Can you guess who it's for?
Take a look behind the door!

# Where's Kitty?

Where's Kitty,
Where's that cat?
I left her sitting
On the mat.

But she went . . .

*under* the table

*through* the socks

*over* the dustpan

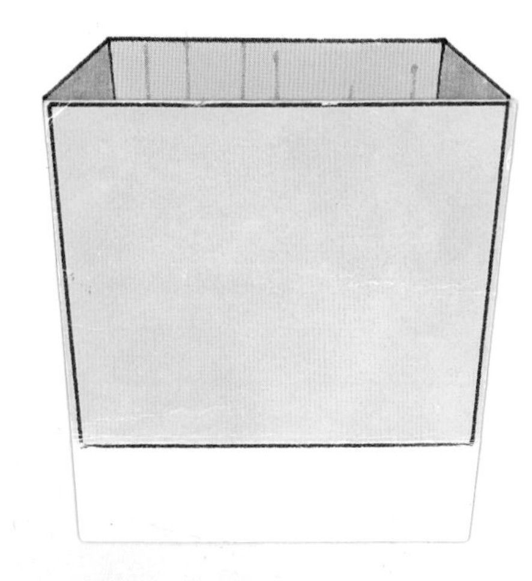

and *into* the box!

# Mary's Lamb

Mary had a little lamb,
Its fleece was white as snow.
And everywhere that Mary went,
The lamb was sure to go.

# Naughty Henry

Henry's been a naughty boy!
He chewed and chewed
My favourite toy!

# Hen and Duck

On the farm there's

a hen . . . and a duck.

The duck has three ducklings.

How many chicks has the hen?

What? Did you say three?
You'd better count again!

# The Kangaroo

Here's a bouncy animal . . .

Bounce, bounce, bounce,
She's a bouncing kangaroo.
She bounces everywhere,
And so does baby, too!

# Hungry Lions

This lion has had his dinner.
He says “Mmmm.”

This lion is hungry. He says “Grr.”

This lion is very hungry. He says “GRRR.”

This lion is *extremely* hungry.
He says . . .